PHONICS CHAP

# The Puppet Club

by Mike Thaler
and Janelle Cherrington
Illustrated by Ana López Escrivá

## Scholastic Inc.
**New York   Toronto   London   Auckland   Sydney**

Copyright © 1998 by Scholastic Inc.
Scholastic *Phonics Chapter Books* is a trademark of Scholastic Inc.
All rights reserved. Published by Scholastic Inc.
Printed in the U.S.A.
ISBN 0-590-76456-X
11 12 13 14 15     04 03 02 01 00

# Dear Teacher/Family Member,

**R**esearch has shown that phonics is an essential strategy for figuring out unknown words. Early readers need the opportunity to learn letter sounds and how to blend or put them together to make words. These skills must be practiced over and over again by reading stories containing words with the sounds being taught.

**T**hat's why I'm happy to be an author and Program Coordinator of the **Phonics Chapter Books**. These books provide early readers with playful, fanciful stories in easy-to-manage chapters. More importantly, the words in the stories are controlled for phonics sounds and common sight words. Once sounds and sight words have been introduced, they are continually reviewed and applied in succeeding stories, so children will be able to decode these books—and read them on their own. There is nothing more powerful and encouraging than success.

John Shefelbine
Associate Professor, Reading Education
California State University, Sacramento

# CONTENTS

| Chapter | Page |
|---|---|

 # 1 Jane and Jake

This is a tale about Jane and her little brother, Jake. Jane and Jake like to tell jokes.

One time a big gift box came for them. It had puppets in it, and it had a kit to make a big puppet stage.

"Look at these nice puppets, Jane! I see a dog, a cat, a pig, and a bug. I like the bug," said Jake.

"But what will we do with this big thing, Jake?" Jane asked.

"We can write a play," said Jake. "Then we can do a puppet show. I have a pen."

Jane said, "OK. Write <u>The Race</u>."

As she spoke, Jane got the pig and cat puppets.

"Hmm," she said. "A pig, a cat, a dog, and a bug. Let me think."

Jake said, "The pig says something about having a race. The one who comes in last wins."

"Yes. That's nice, Jake! Then the pig says 1, 2, 3, STOP!" said Jane.

Jake and Jane kept at it until they had a script.

### The Race

by Jane and Jake

Pig:  Let's have a race. The one who comes in last wins. 1, 2, 3, STOP!

(They all sit.)

Dog:    The sun is hot.

Cat:    Let's sit in the shade.

Bug:    Let's have some cake.

Dog:    It is late.

Cat:    Let's take a nap.

Pig:    We all win the race.
        We all come in last!

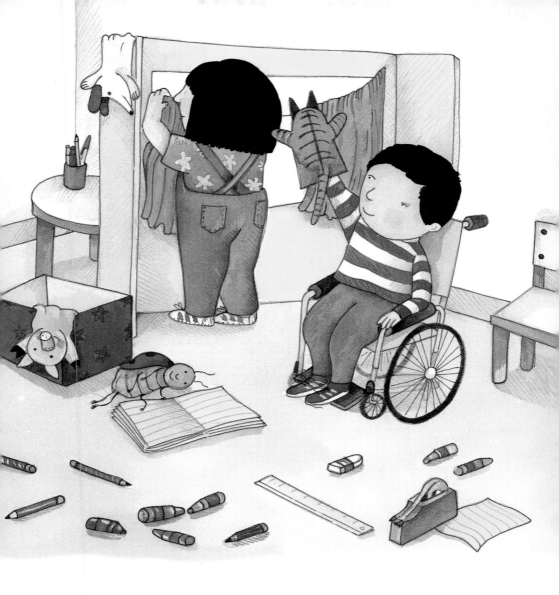

"I like that," Jane said. "This is fun."

"I think so, too," said Jake. "Let's make
the stage and show Mom and Dad.
We can see if they like it."

# 2 A Good Team

Jane and Jake made the stage and let Mom read the script. She said she liked it a lot. So did Jake's friend Mike.

"I think I have some puppets," Mike said. "Can I help with the show?"

Jane said yes, so Mike went home to get his puppets. He had a sheep and a bird.

"Nice puppets," said Jake.

Mike was good with jokes, too. This time the three of them made up the script.

### When a Sheep Can't Sleep
by Mike, Jake, and Jane

Sheep:  Dog, I can't sleep.

Dog:    Take a seat and read.

Sheep:  Cat, I can't sleep.

Cat:    So eat a meal.

Sheep:  I need to sleep, Bird.

Bird:   Go sit in a tree.

Sheep: I can't sleep, Pig.

Pig: Keep your feet in some mud.

Sheep: I can't sleep, Bug.

Bug: Well I can, so leave me alone.

Dog: What do you do if you can't
sleep, Sheep?

Sheep: I count my friends.
One, two, three . . .

(Sheep sleeps.)

All: He can count on us!

(They all go to sleep.)

"That's neat!" said Mike. "We could make a good team!"

# 3 A Breeze

"I like these scripts," said Jake. "Let's write what happens next."

"OK," said Jane. "They all go to sleep. Then what?"

As Jane said this, her friend Beth came. "They dream," Beth said. "You go to sleep and then you dream."

"Yes!" said Mike. "They all dream!"

"Nice work, Beth. That was a big help," Jake said.

"So what is all this?" asked Beth.

Jane said, "We write scripts for puppet shows!"

"I have a frog puppet. Can I help?" asked Beth.

Jake picked up his pen to write.

**Dreams**

by Beth, Mike, Jane, and Jake

(Sheep and his friends wake up.)

Sheep:  I had a dream!

Pig:    What was it about?

Sheep:  I was in a tree, and a bee
was on a green leaf.
The bee said, "Be brave
and look at me." I said "No."
And then he bit me!

Bird:    In my dream, I WAS a leaf
in a tree.

Dog: In my dream, I had a bone to eat.

Frog: In my dream, I had a drink of fresh iced tea.

Bug: In my dream, I gave a speech.

Sheep: About what?

Bug: About gumdrops and dots.

Cat: I often dream of cream, but I did not have a dream.

Sheep: You can have mine.

Cat: No thanks. You can keep it.

"That was a breeze!" said Beth.

# 4 ★ Things Click

"It was a piece of cake!" said Jane. "These are good scripts for puppet shows. We work well as a team!"

"Piece of cake," said Jake. "I like it. That's the name of the next script."

Mike said, "No. I think <u>Bake a Cake</u> is good."

"<u>Bake a Cake</u> it is," said Beth.

**Bake a Cake**

by Jane, Jake, Beth, and Mike

Dog: I have a plan. Let's bake a cake.

Sheep: What would you like
on the cake, Dog?

Dog: I would like a nice
clean bone on the cake.

Sheep: What would you like
on the cake, Cat?

Cat: I would flip for some
cream on the cake.

Sheep: What would you
like on the cake, Pig?

Pig: I would like some thick
black mud on the cake.

Sheep: What would you like
on the cake, Bug?

Bug: I would like many,
many blades of grass.

Sheep: What would you like
on the cake, Frog?

Frog: Could I have a bug
on the cake?

Bug: I am a bug. That's not nice!

Sheep: Let's blend the mix and
bake the cake.

21

Pig:     When can we have it?

Sheep:   When it fluffs up.

Cat:     It will be a good cake!

Bug:     It will be a big cake!

Dog:     It will be a fine cake!

Sheep:   At last! It is time to take
         the cake out!

         (They all clap.)

Pig:     Let's all take a big bite.

Dog:     But where is Bird?

Cat:     He is home.

Sheep:   We could save some cake
         for him, just a little slice.

All:     Yes! He eats like a bird.

# 5 Good Stuff

"This is good stuff!" Mike said. "I think this could be a nice puppet show."

"I think so, too," said Beth. "Can we write a little bit more, so it will be more like a play?"

Just as Beth said that, her friend Steve came. Steve lived just down the block.

"What's up?" Steve asked. "I see puppets, a stage, scripts, and all of you. Is this a puppet club or something?"

"The Puppet Club!" said Jake. "Yes. That's just what this is!"

"Can I help, too?" Steve asked. "It looks like fun. Which puppet can I use?"

### The Snake

by The Puppet Club

Sheep: What would you do if
a snake came to steal
some of this cake?

Bug: I would stand up and be
as big as I could.

Cat: I would give the snake some
cake. Then I would go to sleep.

Bird: I would go up in the tree.

25

Dog:      I would get a stick.

Frog:     I would get a stone.

Pig:      I would make a plan.

Sheep:   Then what would you do?

Bug:      I would step on it.

Bird:     I would snap at it.

Cat:      I would still be sleeping.

Dog:     I would stand on it.

Frog:    I would stomp on it.

Pig:     I would spin on it until it was
         a spot.

Sheep:   Look down. I think I see a snake.

All:     We have to leave!

         (They all run fast.)

# 6 What's Next?

Steve said, "We need an ending.
We can't just let them run out like that."

"Let's think for a little while,"
said Jane.

"When they stop, Dog could ask
if the snake chased them," Beth said.

"OK. Let's see if that will work,"
said Mike.

# Whistle

by The Puppet Club

(The seven friends have just
run a mile to escape a snake.)

All:     Wheeze, wheeze, wheeze!

Dog:     Did the snake chase us?

Pig:     Check and see.

Sheep:   I did. It was not a snake.
         It was just a stick.

Cat:     Let's go. I need some lunch.

Sheep:   We can whistle while we go.

Cat:     I can't whistle, but I can whine.

Pig:     I can wheeze.

Bird:    I can tweet.

Dog:     I can whimper.

Bug: I can squeak.

Frog: I can do all those things.
Which one is best?

Sheep: I will teach you to whistle.
Puff out your chests like this.
One, two, three!

All: (At the same time) Whistle!
Whine! Wheeze! Tweet!
Whimper! Squeak! Ribbit!

Sheep: That was nice. It just needs
a little work.

All: We all won a race.
We all had a dream.
We all had some cake.
We all ran from a snake.
And we all can whistle!

Sheep: (With a big smile) Yes!

"That was fun, but I hope it's not the end of our puppet club," said Beth.

"No," said Mike. "We can meet all the time."

"We can write more stuff," Jake said.

"We can get more friends to help us," said Steve.

"We can even make more puppets," Jane said. "This is The Puppet Club!"

# PHONICS

## Decodable Words With the Phonic Elements

**1**

**a-e**
came
Jane
late
shade
tale

**e-e**
these

**i-e**
like
time

**-ace**
race

**-ake**
cake
Jake
make
take

**-oke**
jokes
spoke

**-ice**
nice

**2**

**e**
he
she
we

**ea**
leave
meal
read
team

**-eat**
eat
neat
seat

**ee**
feet
keep
need
Sheep
sleep
three
tree

**3**

**r-blends**
brave
breeze
cream
dream
drink
fresh
green
tree
gumdrops

**4**

**l-blends**
black
blades
blend
clap
clean
click
flip
fluffs
plan
slice

**5**

**s-blends**
sleep
snake
snap
spin
spot
stand
steal
step
Steve
stick
still
stomp
stone
stuff
asked
fast
just

**6**

**ch**
chase
check
chests
lunch
teach

**sh**
Sheep

**th**
that
them
things
think
this
three
Beth

**wh**
what's
wheeze
when
which
while
whine